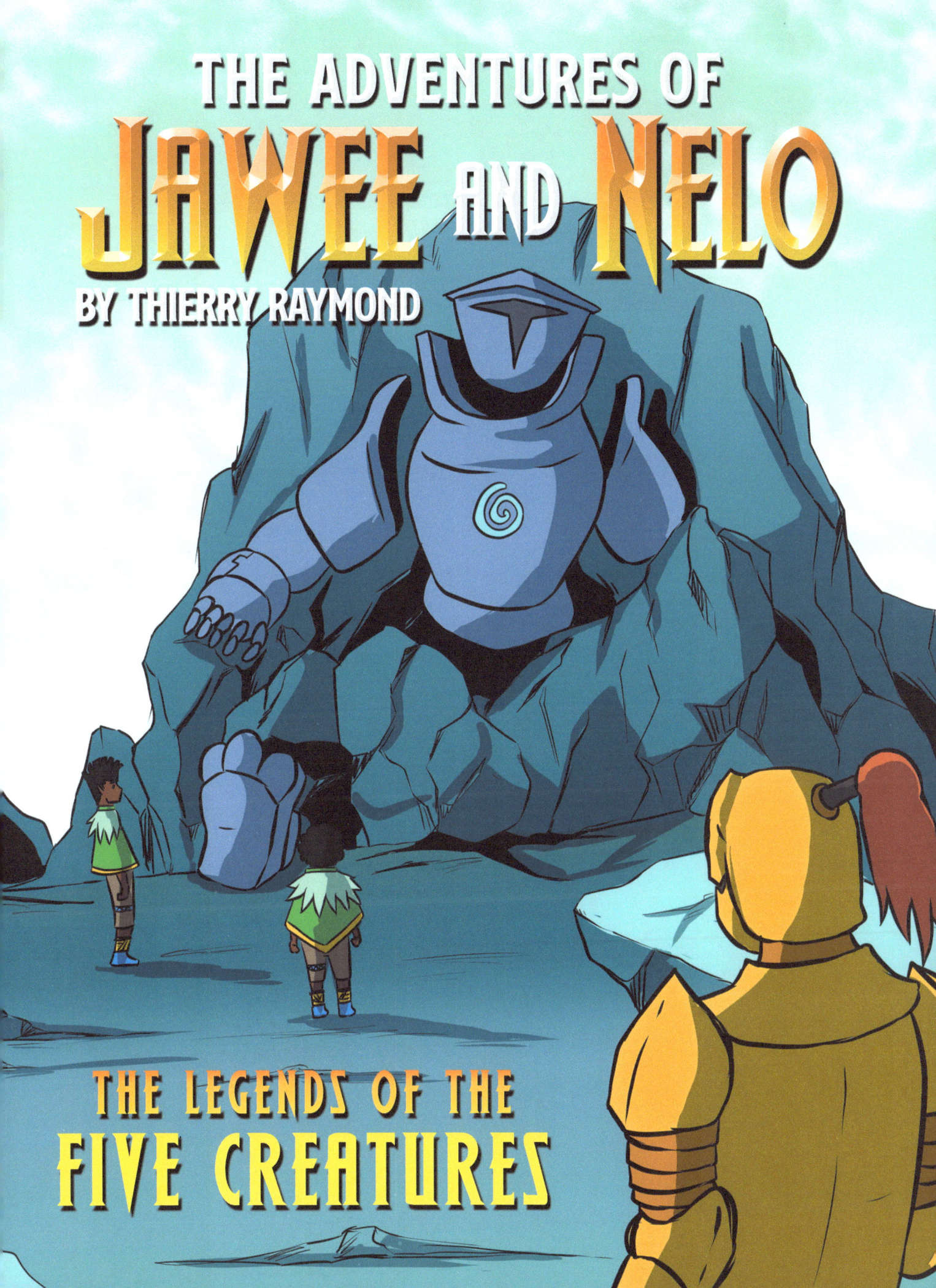

Copyright © 2023 by Thierry Raymond.

All rights reserved. No part of this book may be reproduced in any form or by any electronic or mechanical means, including information storage and retrieval systems, without permission in writing from the publisher, except by reviewers, who may quote brief passages in a review.

This publication contains the opinions and ideas of its author. It is intended to provide helpful and informative material on the subjects addressed in the publication. The author and publisher specifically disclaim all responsibility for any liability, loss, or risk, personal or otherwise, which is incurred as a consequence, directly or indirectly, of the use and application of any of the contents of this book.

WRITERS REPUBLIC L.L.C.
515 Summit Ave. Unit R1
Union City, NJ 07087, USA

Website: *www.writersrepublic.com*
Hotline: *1-877-656-6838*
Email: *info@writersrepublic.com*

Ordering Information:
Quantity sales. Special discounts are available on quantity purchases by corporations, associations, and others. For details, contact the publisher at the address above.

Library of Congress Control Number: 2023901139
ISBN-13: 979-8-88810-443-9 [Paperback Edition]
979-8-88810-444-6 [Digital Edition]

Rev. date: 02/06/2023

THE ADVENTURES OF JAWEE AND NELO

This took me over a year to finish and many times I wanted to quit but I kept thinking of my initial purpose to write this book and kept going. Sometimes I was bombarded with ideas and inspiration. I'm very glad I was able to complete the book. I'm also positive about the entertainment it will give to the reader.

—Thierry Raymond

CHAPTER 1

The story begins in an underground city, deeply hidden inside the jungle undisturbed and alarmed by the modern day 21st century civilisation.

This is an ancient world, full of magic and customs unknown to a regular person.

Let me introduce you to the Laska. They are part of the Green tribe in Tikki.

Tikki has three worlds, which means it's located in three places on your map, stretching from Africa through Asia.

These three worlds consist of three tribes, each attributed to their own colour. Green of course is Laska; Gold is the colour of the tribe called the Mulon and lastly Red which belongs to the tribe called Shama.

This great story is about an evil corporation that plans to take over the world by raiding and stealing its resources for fuel and power. One man named Cliff Robinson, employed by Doorcom, would spend days and nights and week after week, searching relentlessly for a lost city. Finally he discovers one. Cliff gets a team of archaeologists and laborers to make an expedition to ultimately explore the sites. Upon arrival, he discovers a rich land full of weird insects and wild animals.

Jawee and Nelo are playing tag and picking berries in a field nearby. Grazing the land, they are shocked when they stumble upon a crowd of laborers and archaeologists. Jawee and Nelo, being from Laska, possess powers that can control birds, and can make plants grow instantly.

Each inhabitant of Laska has been taught how to control birds and as well as make plants grow instantly. It is part of their education growing up in Laska.

Nelo is a clumsy little one; and he slips and breaks a branch. A few laborers notice him and immediately after they spot Jawee trying to signal Nelo to be quiet. The laborers chase down and capture the two little ones to finally bring them to Cliff Robinson.

Cliff is fascinated by the appearance of the two. They look wild and awkwardly alien to our societies and civilization. He decides to have a chat with the two while they're being held captive inside the encampment.

Jawee and Nelo are dressed in feathered clothes. Jawee has long hair and Nelo has it short. They both look skinny, but well-shaped. Two oddly looking, cute little fellows observe Cliff as he puffs on his cigar.

Cliff gathers his crew and reinforces his search for this wonderful lost ancient city. He figures these two look so strange, he suspects they must belong to an ancient tribe. Doorcom will surely give him a healthy paycheck if he discovers Laska.

Most of his coworkers made fun of him when he spoke of his expedition to his boss Mr. Ford.

Mr. Ford is an evil, greedy corporate guru. He is a multi-billionaire business owner. He owns Doorcom and has no heart for competition. Therefore has little respect for human life I'd say.

Cliff is a good man and shows both concern and worry for these children who appear alone and without supervision. He decides to call for an orphanage. He only has a few days left in his expedition.

Jawee and Nelo are joyful and playing around with the laborers. They are oblivious to a lot of things, but they do notice the strange appearance of these men who are of course very different from the inhabitants of Laska. Laska is a city made of crystals. They are not visible from a distance, but you can see crystals sprinkled all over the pasturage in the land of Laska full of magic and mysteries unknown to our world. Yet, it is hidden right next to us. This different world the two boys are part of is called Tikki and is the healing of the planet, the source of life and connection to the mysteries of heaven.

Suddenly, Cliff stumbles upon and dicovers a crystal road near a river.

"I found Laska" he screams in excitement!

He sees a valley underneath the ground leading to the lake with a bridge showing a city.

"What a wonder," says the crew as they stare and approach the city. Legend has it that one day there will be outsiders who will enter Laska and by doing so will awaken the five sleeping creatures resting in the waters of Laska. These creatures will go on to begin what is the end of our own world.

If you ever have the misfortune to gaze at one of these creatures, you will turn to stone. The five sleeping creatures are gigantic stone heads with hidden mechanical bodies. No one knows the creator of these creatures. Perhaps it is from an ancient city buried underneath the ocean or from Gods? Could it be the creation of a great wizard? No one in Laska knows of its mysteries. Cliff explores the valley with the crew, slowly heading towards the magical Laska.

Jawee is very aware of the legends of the five creatures. He isn't the brightest child in the city, but he is concerned about Cliff and his crew. He decides to make up a plan to prevent them from arriving. Who knows if the legends are true and what can happen to his world and our world.

Jawee signals Nelo quietly. A noise is heard coming from the North, East side of the road. Cliff hears it and leaps forth fearfully. Branches are heard breaking and the ground quivers. The crew sets up and mobilizes for battle. Suddenly, bushes and bushes of leaves spin forth all around them. Jawee winks at Nelo with a boastful smile.

He is using his powers to shake the leaves. Some skill he has acquired over the years. The crew bites the bait and all one by one start to panic. They take off running, backtracking on their footsteps. Cliff is trying desperately to control and calm his crew, but with no avail. There is a reason behind the actions of Jawee: prudence is a virtue and he believes it is better to be safe than sorry. Who knows what will happen if these creatures wake up? They are so ancient, they are said to be three billion human years old.

Some things mankind cannot understand, it is knowledge that only the inhabitants of Laska conceive. The elders have warned the villages about these creatures and speak of prophecies of old. If they are to wake up, it will be the end of mankind as we know it. The gates of magic will unleash intertwining with the normal world and the unknown world.

After dawn the crew and Clifford transport the two like cargo. They take Jawee and Nelo back to the ship, leading them through the city where normal civilization lies. This begins our story and this big adventure.

The crew arrives near the airport in Tanzania. They load the plane and get ready to head back home to Canada. In the meantime Jawee is sitting down in wonder, trying to figure out what is a plane and where he and his companion will end up. Nelo is just going around careless and oblivious. He is eating all the food he comes across.

"Time to leave", says Cliff.

"We are all set", responds one of his loyal staff members.

Everyone, one by one enter the plane and get seated. When the plane takes off, Jawee and Nelo begin to start chanting and dancing. They mistake a plane for a giant phoenix and in Laska it is polite to chant for a phoenix if he lets you fly with him. The crew looks at them with confused and amazed faces. This is going to be a long flight, says Clifford. Clifford locks himself in his cabin. He sits down and drowns himself in paperwork, his face looks fatigued, and he is exhausted. Clifford sets his chair back as he reclines and picks up a frame; it's a picture of his wife Rose and his daughter Kia. He stares at it, he misses them very much. Finally they arrive and land safely. They are greeted by an army of security accompanied by Mr. Ford, the evil corporate guru. He stands there, anxious to see what his employee Clifford has discovered during that trip. His lips are salivating like he is ready to eat all the information. Expansion is what he wants and he will stop at no cost to obtain it. Jawee and Nelo are taken to an underground base in Mr. Ford's estate. They hop into a shuttle and can see construction as they slowly descend down a great valley. Cliff organized a big presentation showing the landscape, the herbs and vegetation including some various species of wild animals he and the crew encountered. He set up a great show for his boss Mr. Ford.

Ford of course has a dark stare and although he is pleased, looks unsurprised and impressed by the presentation. Cliff gets disappointed and immediately signals a few men to set out and go fetch for Jawee and Nelo.

"And now for what you've been all waiting for" – shouts Clifford!

The two make their appearance puzzled and all confused. It's as if time stopped when Mr. Ford sees them. His arms and knees quiver as thoughts of glory spiral inside his mind. Cliff is very pleased by Ford's reaction but then he suddenly feels disturbed and uncomfortable because he has sympathy for the two. He is worried about what will happen to Jawee and Nelo in the future. Ford gathers a team of scientists to conduct tests on the two odd little ones. When the scientist reaches for Nelo, a thunderous sound is heard all across the lab. It was Jawee, he made a hard gesture that caused the whole room to turn green and full of vegetation. So much so you can't see past it. The staffs are taken by fright and yell in terror as they run back and forth across the room. Nelo laughs at them and climbs a tree. He is very agile and discreet therefore goes undetected. The ground trembles and swirls followed by trees that spring forth from the ground.

"How is this possible?" exclaimed Ford.

In great wonder he watches his laboratory get demolished. The two have disappeared and are nowhere to be found. A gas pipe bursts and ignites a large fire that slowly rises above the room.

CHAPTER 2

"The security system is no longer functional" says a scientist to Clifford.

"We must evacuate sir". Clifford ignores the scientist and has his mind elsewhere; he keeps shouting Jawee and Nelo name from side to side then zig-zags across the room.

He searches relentlessly for them while everyone gets evacuated from the site. A sudden explosion happens, causing Clifford to fall down and stick his foot in between two rocks. As he falls, he knocks his head pretty badly causing him to become dizzy and light-headed. Jawee spots him from afar; he and Nelo were making their escape but couldn't help but feel compassion for the middle aged man. They reach out and save him before the fire engulfs the whole place. As they pull him to safety he faints. The two carry him up the valley very carefully while they stealth, hiding from unwanted attention. Hours go by with no sign that Clifford will awake from his coma. Finally a movement occurs followed by a cough. Jawee and Nelo look at each other and chuckle. Clifford Robinson's eyesight gradually comes back to normal as he yawns and stretches. He is full of gratitude and thanks them. Surprisingly the two saved his life. He feels indebted so he decides and also vouches that he will bring these guys back to Laska where they belong.

"Where and how can he bring them to safety?" debate's Clifford with a concerned stare.

He comes to the conclusion that he will sneak them to him and his wife's house. It's a nice dwelling near the lake in a small town with a closed community. The type of people who reside there you may consider "bougie", with gardens and picket fences. He plans to discreetly hide Jawee and Nelo in his cabin in the backyard.

"Should he even tell his wife Rose about the two?" questions Clifford.

She was really angry with him when he had his brother live with them for one week. His brother ruined a lot of furniture and made a huge mess. Cliff, Jawee and Nelo quietly arrive unspotted nor heard by anyone. Not even his neighbors, including his wife and his daughter Kia, notice them. Luckily it's dawn and the sun hasn't risen yet. They install themselves in the cabin, covered and well hidden in the attic. Clifford walks home and enters the house languidly.

His wife greets him in the kitchen. She is very busy cooking a mouthwatering flavorful meal for her daughter Kia who is watching TV in the living room. When she spots her father, she immediately jumps up with a smile screaming, "Pappy". That's a nickname Kia gave her dad a while back. Rose, her mother tells her to sit down and that the meal is ready.

In the meantime lots of strange things are happening in the cabin. Jawee and Nelo have discovered tools and a lawn mower. Curiosity overwhelms them and they start to touch the tools. Cliff is at the table with family when lots of loud consecutive noises are heard. Rose and Kia are startled by the sound. Cliff interrupts and calms them by saying there was an earthquake announcement today not too far from town; it probably made itself here. The two girls seem to buy his story. Cliff luckily gets to breath as he pants for air with a little bit of sweat dripping down his forehead. He must discipline and control the two, he thinks to himself. After dining, Cliff leaves the table and waltzes in on Jawee and Nelo. They abruptly stop what they're doing.

"What a mess!" says Clifford in disappointment. He decides to install a camera system after having a long talk with the two strangers from Laska. They don't seem to understand anything. While all this is happening, Kia Cliff's daughter is quietly relaxing upstairs in her room. She has a very nice view of the cabin. Sometimes when Kia gets bored at night she sneaks out of her room and sets up in the cabin. Kia is a bit Crafty and collects scrap yard parts of different items, sometimes she tries to build bikes and sleds, skateboards and go-karts. Some girls pick on her at school because she is a bit of a weirdo. She doesn't follow the crowd, therefore has no friends but she does own two birds, two parakeets that she has named Loco and Simka. They keep her company in her room and she is still trying to teach them to talk. She loves them and they love her. They have a bond probably because she feeds them very well.

Cliff heads back home tired. He gets ready to go to bed and he performs his routine clean up while his wife Rose awaits for him in bed. As the night falls, Nelo feels restless; he decides to get out of the cabin and go for a swim in the lake nearby. Unfortunately Kia hears the noise. She looks out her window and sees nothing but Kia is curious and decides to investigate. She also wants to touch and modify some scraps she has left in the cabin. She slowly makes her way there while Jawee is asleep and Nelo is outside in the lake.

An air of suspense takes place as she enters the dark room. She rattles a chair while she reaches for a light switch. Jawee staggers and wakes up suddenly. He immediately hides while Kia goes on to play with her tools and gadgets, unbothered and oblivious to the presence of Jawee.

Jawee stares at her in wonder, staying well put in a stealth position. A few minutes pass without interruption. It's a dark night full of stars and all you can hear are crickets. Meanwhile, Nelo has finished taking his swim and exits the water with a smile. He is very acrobatic. He spins and it only takes him three flips to get back to the cabin. What happens if he enters abruptly without warning? Surely he will be spotted by Kia. This will undoubtedly cause a big change in her perception of life. Of course Nelo is very clumsy, so he storms in the cabin like a fool. The camera is running and the door is opened. Kia is astounded and they both stare at each other in shock. The two gaze at each other from head to toe, scanning and analyzing each other's appearance.

"Who are you?" asks Kia.

"I am Nelo", he answers. They converse and exchange information and that is when Jawee feels comfortable enough to exit his hiding place. Kia is frightened and leaps backwards, confused.

"Hi I'm Jawee his brother" exclaims Jawee.

They all spend the night talking and comparing the differences between her world and their world. The next day, early in the morning, Cliff has to go to work. He has no clue of the kids' encounter. He's prepared a meal for Jawee and Nelo and discreetly makes his way to the cabin to deliver it. The two greet him, but he is in a hurry and has to go. Cliff is worried about work and what Mr. Ford will say. It's a big loss and most likely Mr. Ford will be furious. Kia watches her father Clifford depart.

As he enters his car, she slowly makes her way out of the cabin. Nelo and Jawee are still sleeping but are awakened by her thump when she opens the door. They spend time with each other laughing and enjoying themselves. Kia came up with an idea. She suggests they come into her room and visit her birds Loco and Simka. Jawee and Nelo are excited and agree by showing her a nod. They make their way to the house camouflaging behind the bushes. They finally arrive there without her mom noticing a thing.

Once Jawee and Nelo make contact with the two birds Loco and Simka, a connection happens. A very, very strange connection happens. Something that Kia has no idea of. She is unaware that the inhabitants of Laska can control and talk to birds. Not only can they do this, but with practice, they can also see from the birds' view.

Suddenly something amazing happens. Simka and Loco start to speak. Kia miraculously could understand what was being said. The birds are arguing about keeping one side of the cage clean. Then they murmur, "She's back and she's with weirdos!"

Now everyone in the room is shocked and confused except for Jawee and Nelo who quickly come with the answers to everyone's confusion. They teach Kia a lesson on the history of Tikki and the place they are from – Laska, a mythical, magical land of wonders. The story unfolds and during the conversation a bond is made amongst everyone. They laugh and have a merry time.

But not too far away, a very sinister shadow lurks around. Mr. Pho is the loyal assistant of Mr. Ford. He ordered some agents to spy on Clifford once he found out about his discovery. They installed a wiretap system at his location. Unfortunately, the security camera Clifford installed in their cabin was compromised. Mr. Pho, a dreadful man, this whole time was watching, plotting the worst for the group of kids. He also can't wait to inform Mr. Ford of Clifford's betrayal.

CHAPTER 3

A gusty wind followed by a thunderstorm starts to build under the skies of our friendly characters. Jawee looks at the window while it starts to drizzle with small raindrops hitting the window screen.

"Let's get you guys back in the cabin", says Kia, a bit worried.

In the meantime, Clifford arrives at Doorcom and passes his ID card through the security scanner and makes it on time to sit at his office. Mr. Ford calls out for him on the telecom within only a few minutes of his arrival. Cliff makes his way to the top floor of the building, that's where Mr. Ford's office is located. He has a view of the city by his window and that's where he strategizes and plans.

Mr. Ford greets Cliff with an angry tone, he's enraged. He interrogates Clifford and wants to know what transpired the day of the event. This cold old man hasn't even asked Clifford if he is ok, he is only concerned about his benefits and wants his merchandise.

"The future of Doorcom is at stake" says Mr. Ford!

This man has an eerie look to him and it's horrifying to think that he only sees Jawee and Nelo as merchandise. Cliff is very clever and finds a way to calm and reassure Mr. Ford. He promises him he will undertake another expedition but this time at his own expense. He must not let Mr. Ford know about their whereabouts.

Unfortunately for Cliff, there is an elevator that swings open and Mr. Pho exits the door. He slowly makes his way to the top floor, anxious to inform his boss of his discovery. He must tell him he found the two boys from Laska. Not too far away, droplets of rain continue to fall on the roof of the cabin. The kids are now seated and Kia is teaching them how to play cards as she shuffles the deck.

During their fun time, Jawee gets up and secludes himself in a sector of the cabin. Kia eventually is curious and wonders what he is doing. She finds Jawee motionless in a sitting position similar to a lotus. She turns to Nelo with a questioning look. Nelo explains to her about their power. They require recharging and therefore must meditate for one hour each day. Without their daily meditation, they will be unable to access their gift and have the ability to control birds as well as make trees and plants of all types grow. An aura glimmers from Jawee's body as he sits motionless with no sound. She marvels at him with a twinkle. How amazing must Laska be?

Meanwhile, in Mr. Ford's office, Clifford is handed a new assignment. This time Mr. Ford threatens him and warns him that he will sue him for every penny he owns if he fails. Cliff cannot fail this assignment; he has a family to take care of. Lastly, Mr. Pho finally walks in; great trouble awaits Clifford.

Mr. Pho all excited gives an evil smirk to Cliff and then says eagerly, "I have important news to give you sir!"

"What is it?", responds Mr. Ford anxiously.

"I know the whereabouts of the children from Laska."

Mr. Pho goes on to expose Cliff and tells Mr. Ford about his betrayal, about how the kids are hidden in his cabin and how he cleverly put his house on watch. Cliff is now terrified but mostly worried about his family and also for Jawee and Nelo. He gets angry at Mr. Pho for putting his house on watch and spying on him. Mr. Ford interjects with a loud voice full of anger. He commands his security to take a hold of Cliff.

In surprise, Clifford yells "You can't do that!"

Security advances on him and grabs him violently. They take a hold of him and bring him into a secluded room in Mr. Ford's building. Mr. Pho has a grin as he watches the guards manhandle Clifford. Ford gathers a team of security to zone in on Jawee and Nelo's location. He gets ready to capture the magical boys from Laska. You can hear loud engine noise as the trucks and cars get ready to ambush Clifford's house. Ford, this lazy old man, hops on a helicopter, following the team of security. Clifford is restrained then tied to a desk bolted strongly to the floor. Unfortunately there is nothing he can do to help or warn his family.

Jawee and Nelo are with Kia still playing cards, enjoying the rainy day. Suddenly they hear noise followed by a flapping sound coming closer and closer. Nelo sticks his head out the window and spots a helicopter. To his left there is an onslaught of cars driving on their way. Actions must be undertaken, Nelo thinks to himself. Kia panics and is very worried.

"What about my mother? She's at the house!" she screams.

Jawee places his hand on her to calm her down, then he looks at the floor. Slowly the floor begins to tremble, then a passageway starts to appear as a leaf with roots and branches start to push the ground aside to create an underground tunnel. Jawee grabs Kia's hand and they enter it with Nelo following behind. Nelo whistles, then one by one, birds of all types start to come near Kia's house.

Rose is actually resting and having a small nap. She enjoys a nap on a rainy day. She finds it soothing and very relaxing to sleep to the sound of raindrops. While Rose, Kia's mother, is asleep, tall birds take a hold of her and carry her to the window. Then suddenly with one leap they take her off the ground and fly her up, lifting her up through the sky. Kia witnesses this with amazement.

"They will carry her to safety," says Jawee.

Mr. Ford's team arrives speeding but still too late. By the time they get to location the kids have covered too much ground. They are no longer on site. Even Rose is transported and put down delicately on a park bench. Mr. Ford and Mr. Pho enters the cabin with their security team armed. They search the place and only find cards with a joker on the table. Even the tunnel is no longer there. They then make their way anxiously to Clifford house. There too they find no one. Mr. Ford's face turns red with anger and he looks at Mr. Pho.

While all this action is going on, Clifford is segregated and alone in isolation. He is suffering from psychological trauma. He cannot think of a solution to escape and is very worried for his family as well as the kids. He imagines many bad scenarios all ending with a very bad outcome.

Rose wakes up on the park bench. There is an old poor woman with a basket resting near her with a blanket. Rose slowly regains consciousness at which point she begins to question her own sanity. She stares at the old lady as she walks away. Still confused but nonchalantly she brushes the thoughts away. She is not yet aware of Jawee and Nelo and their magical powers.

Meanwhile under great stress, Kia is trying to find a solution to figure out where her friends Jawee and Nelo can have a place to stay. She doesn't travel much without her parents and she doesn't know who would take her in. Kia only remembers where her clumsy uncle Lexton resides. Every time he would visit her house, he'd manage to break furniture, always falling and not paying attention. He would always boast about his accolades and mention stories about his life with her dad. She is hesitant but concludes and decides they should go and settle there.

Kia makes the boys take a train to her uncle Lexton's household. They observe the crowd of people in the train station as well as its architecture. Not only do Jawee and Nelo start to love the world of humans, but they are becoming accustomed to it. To their surprise as they get near Lexton's neighborhood, they notice lots of littering, open garbage, strange people, bums and broken tall buildings. Lexton's neighborhood is far from similar to his brother Clifford neighborhood. It's not upscale like Kia's home and it's much more busier.

They arrive at his building and ring his buzzer. No response while she continuously buzzes. When Kia resigns the alarm door awkwardly rings. The kids enter and make their way towards

Lexton's apartment. A strange silence lingers as they approach and knock on his door. No answer from Lexton again.

Lexton is a very paranoid fellow. Not only does he live in an impoverished project area but he also owes a lot of money to numerous people. He spends his nights gambling and borrowing money from different loan sharks. Lexton takes a peep through the hole and opens the door abruptly, reaches out and pulls the three kids in the apartment.

"What are you doing here Kia?" says Lexton looking back and forth before he slams the door behind them.

"We need your help", responds Kia.

After a few minutes of introduction, the kids sit her uncle Lexton down to explain to him the events that occurred at her house. Lexton pops a bottle of alcohol open and stressfully begins to guzzle a few shots as he hears the story.

Then he gets up with a moronic look and says, "We can be millionaires if we film a documentary on Jawee and Nelo, it will make the news".

With an embarrassed and ashamed look, Kia waves no at her uncle and goes on to lecture him. He apologizes and seeks to redeem himself by offering cookies and treats to the kids. Of course they accept it, they love cookies and treats. Lexton used to be a DJ in his neighborhood, so he is very popular. Unfortunately he has a bad reputation because he is unreliable and owes a lot of people some money. Despite how incoherent he is, he would be the right candidate to make Jawee and Nelo famous, something that Kia does not want and I'm sure her father Clifford wouldn't either.

Impulsively, Lexton realizes that this whole current episode that happened to the kids may have something to do with his brother Clifford and his job at Doorcom. Lexton is aware of Mr. Ford and his sinister ambitious mind. He and Clifford have spoken about it in the past. He decides to mention it to Kia and in return she freaks out. They determine they must find out if Clifford is safe and they should call his cell phone. The phone rings a few times, but ends with no answer. Kia gets more and more worried.

FLAP FLAP FLAP

Lexton, Kia, Jawee and Nelo create a diagram in order to set up a plan of action. They decide they must sneak in and invade Doorcom just to observe the area and see if there is suspicious activity. Jawee quietly whistles and signals Loco and Simka to fly their way to Doorcom; they will be the eyes of the group. They speedily take off in the air, swirling and spinning around. Nelo starts to laugh excessively, so much so that Kia and Lexton get annoyed by it and ask him why he is laughing.

That's when he replies, "Jawee has sent your birds Loco and Simka to Doorcom; they will take care of the mission and report back to us".

They both approve of what he says and gain confidence.

Meanwhile on Mr. Ford's extensive property, Clifford is slowly falling asleep, fatigued from lack of water. He lies there with his hands tied strongly, against a desk bolted to the floor. What can he do? He has no means to remove a bolt by unscrewing the nut from a bolt with a wrench. Security is walking around in every corner of Mr. Ford's estate. Mr. Ford owns many properties, but this one in particular is private. He made investments in laboratories in hopes of discovering different worlds. His family did not approve of his idea, which is why this place is classified and completely unknown. Scientists of every field practice and do test runs.

The skies are clear now with a few clouds and Simka is hovering and gliding like the wind. Also following behind is his bird friend Loco, whistling as he slashes through the wind. Eventually they arrive in Mr. Ford's estate, drifting above the buildings. They are completely unnoticed given that they are animals and can blend in with nature and the fauna. They fly around searching and scouting the area while fantastically Jawee's eyes can browse and search as well, seeing everything the birds can see.

From Lexton's apartment, he describes in detail to Kia and everyone else what he can spot. They all crouch on Jawee with a countenance of suspense. The tension in the room is palpable. The search for rescue is relentless and the passion coming from Kia motivates the team not to give up. Loco and Simka are triumphant and courageously spot Clifford's leg from a window. They enter it by climbing through a pipe hole from the building. Clifford is unconscious, exhausted and dehydrated, all alone in an empty room with only one desk. Loco and Simka begin to whistle real loud to wake him up. Kia celebrates with great joy with Jawee and Nelo and the crew.

Clifford wakes up to the whistling of the birds. In shock when he notices Loco and Simka he gets confused. How can his little birds from home make it right here, so far from home? He wonders deeply.

Simka says "Hey Cliff wake up you lazy old man!"

Cliff jumps and panics at his words. "You can speak!" Cliff says in astonishment.

"Yes you dummy", Loco replies accompanied by a laugh.

The birds start laughing. This must be related to the boys from Laska, Cliff realizes. It's a rescue mission. The birds untie Clifford's hands by unscrewing the desk vigorously. Free at last he stands up. Sadly on the outside of this room, security guards roam the building and move about the hallways. If they hear or see anything suspicious Clifford is done for it.

CHAPTER 4

Cliff has an idea and has come up with a plan to escape and get out of the room. He whispers his scheme to Loco and Simka.

One guard makes his way down the hallway and begins to hear chirping coming from a room. He follows the sound that leads him to Clifford's room. The guard hesitates before he unlocks the door. When he opens the door he notices Simka on the table chirping and chirping. Next to the bird lies Clifford completely unconscious and tied. Little does he know, Loco is next to the light bulb on the ceiling. He strikes it, causing the room to turn pitch black. Blinded, the guard leaves an open lane for Clifford and Simka to attack. Cliff knocks the guard down causing him to be disabled. They make their getaway and enter the hallway. Jawee and the crew, still in suspense, were watching all along. Kia is getting restless and really anxious to do something. The hallway is heavily guarded and it looks nearly impossible to go by it undetected.

Cliff gets a brilliant idea and decides to put on the unconscious guard uniform. He slips it on then ushers his way into the hallway. Loco and Simka return to the pipe hole to find a new exit; they wish to keep a close eye on Cliff. Patrolling the area are few guards on post. Luckily Clifford walks by them unnoticed. Moisture starts to build as sweat drips down Clifford's forehead because he's very nervous. He surprisingly finesses every security guard making his way to the last exit at the first floor.

Clifford escapes successfully, takes a gasp for air before cracking a smile. Loco and Simka together wait for him outside both standing on a tree branch. Kia and the crew celebrate in Lexton's apartment. It's time for Clifford to get reunited with his daughter after so much trauma. Unfortunately little does everyone know, when Cliff got into a wrestle with Mr. Pho before getting ambushed by security, Mr. Pho slipped a tracking device on Clifford, this clever conniving scientist is always watching and seems to be ten steps ahead of everyone.

Mr. Pho is ready to travel with Mr. Ford but also has a plan. He tells Mr. Ford not to move to action and to leave Clifford to walk freely.

"Doing so, perhaps he will lead us to Laska" says Mr. Pho.

"Let's just keep an eye on him and follow him from a distance," utters Ford with an evil grin. He finds Mr. Pho's plan genius and is well pleased.

Reunited at last, a gathering takes place with cries of joy and sorrow from Clifford and Kia are heard as the two hug each other with love. Jawee and Nelo look at each other and decide to join in; even the birds are moved to tears by such a scene. They all cry out and hug each other with tears of happiness. It's funny to watch. Little do they know this is not the end but instead the beginning of their problems. Clifford doesn't know he is being tracked.

Now that our conglomerate of friends are safe they must find a secure place away from the city to exile. Cliff urgently contacts his wife Rose to make sure she is fine and to warn her of Mr. Ford's evil plan. She has no clue of what has happened and is still confused and wondering whether or not she is going a bit crazy and will have to visit a psychologist.

When Cliff finally explains to her what is going on, the information is so overbearing to Rose that she faints and drops the phone while Cliff is still on the line. Lost in a different world away from home are Jawee and Nelo with no one but themselves from Laska. They are worried and a bit homesick.

Rose awakens from her short slumber and wishes to see Jawee and Nelo. Their outward appearance is mystical, almost unearthly. The inhabitants of Tikki commonly have skins that illuminate when they use their powers. Laska, where Jawee and Nelo are from, have skins that turn Green unlike the inhabitants of Mulon which have skins that turn gold when they engage. Lastly from these magical lands we also have the occupants of Shama whose skins glow slightly Red when they feel the need to use their powers. Rose departs from home and heads through Lexton`s neighborhood on a mission to meet the bizarre, unfamiliar two faces. In the worlds of Jawee and Nelo they all share this illuminating skin appearance and will all die and return to that color designated to them. Rose knows nothing of this world she barely knows how to get around in her own neighborhood without G.P.S.

She arrives at Lexton's when the sun sets and it's almost nightfall. Joint together for days and weeks, our team of family and friends get acquainted with each other by comparing life in Laska to life in our world. They've been traveling and living in different hotels since they all agreed that it wasn't safe to stay in the city. Despite the circumstances, this is Kia's first road trip with her family and fortunately for her she gets to enjoy it with Jawee and Nelo also.

While on the road in the family van they have enjoyed watching the pasturage and grazing animals through the window. Rose has a discussion with Clifford about alerting the authorities of Doorcom and Mr. Ford's illegal master plan. They soon realize it is not a good idea, Doorcom owns a share of practically everything and even the police can't be trusted to some degree. This is why it has been weeks that our crew has been riding on this journey avoiding all unwanted attention.

Sadly they've overlooked the cleverness of Mr. Pho and ignored the fact that they are being watched. Mr. Ford is growing impatient and wants to execute an order to seize all of them. Contrary to his will, Mr. Pho rejects this order and advises Ford not to. It is best for them to remain patient and like a hunter, wait for their prey to get tired. They will lead them to Laska eventually. Mr. Ford is on a quest for power; he will certainly make a huge fortune if he finds Laska. The world would venerate him and mention his achievements in the history books only if he succeeds. They take no action, instead reinforce surveillance on Cliff and his family.

Mr. Pho fashions a robot and programs it to follow the group. He names the robot Axo. The robot is designed with a propulsive system that allows him to fly. This is necessary for him to spy on Cliff and his family without being spotted. The robot sits quiet inside a glass frame full of water, waiting to be activated. Once launched, his arm moves deliberately to salute Mr. Ford. His journey begins to fulfill his mission. He takes off with power on his way to Jawee and Nelo.

CHAPTER 5

Very far away in a distant land unknown to us is an old woman with a vision. The old woman is from Mulon that world next to Laska. Mama Esmelda is her name and she, believe it or not, is the grandmother of Jawee and Nelo. She's been having nightmares and visions of the end of the worlds. She's seen her grandsons in her dreams and grew worried.

When Rose woke up on the park bench, it was her that was watching over her. She is the strange old lady she had encountered. Mama Esmelda has crossed the border between her magical world to our world in hopes to find Jawee and Nelo so she can warn them. A perilous future is ahead for earth and all of humanity. She sensed some magic which led her to follow Rose around from a distance. The time comes for our family to end the road trip. They must return Jawee and Nelo home to Laska; Clifford knows it will be a difficult task because they will be required to board a plane and cross the continent to Africa without being spotted. Although they have driven pretty far away from the city, Cliff and Rose know they can't be too safe and that Mr. Ford is strategic, he may have spies in all of the airports.

Jawee and Nelo unfortunately do not have enough magic to take them there. Not only do they need to recharge but they will not be able to fly above the large ocean for that many days without recharging. They will need a place to land to regain their powers. Kia is a very clever young girl and gets an idea.

"What if we travel by boat?" she suggests.

"Great idea!" says Cliff while he scrolls through ads of boats and cruise ships leaving the country. Observing from afar with robotic limestone eyes is Axo on stealth mode. Our friends are not so safe and being watched while they prepare to travel and pack their bags. Above the robot we find a loving and caring stare from Mama Esmelda. She is fully aware of everything that is going on. In her world the people have built a city under water. Mulon is wondrous and the inhabitants have power over water, they can magnificently control water with their thoughts and fuse with it as well. It's such a great gift, they can also by use of fish, have sound waves. They use fish like people in this world use cell phones strangely.

She is now in our world, Esmelda has her eyes fixated on Axo the robot. She watches with plans to destroy him. When it's morning and the sun hasn't risen yet, Clifford Robinson and the

Robinson family with friends board a ship one by one. Kia carries the birds Loco and Simka in her small bird cage. She hides them with a blanket over the cage while scanning her ticket to enter the ship. Once on board, Cliff and Rose feel a sense of security when the anchor is lifted and the ship prepares to sail. They want Jawee and Nelo to return home safely without jeopardizing the world as we know it. They made a pledge never to follow them and cross the border to Laska. The prophecies might be true; no human should enter the realm of Laska and pass the gates.

Now at the sea, it's a misty sky and the night is falling. Axo has snuck himself in the ship by entering the bottom side of it. The wind blows and the sea level rises causing great waves. The strong winds create severe weather and eventually a storm builds up. Although the ship is of massive dimensions, there is still a big risk it could sink. The captain and his crew desperately make sure there are no areas of the ship flooding. The stability of the ship is at risk and the passengers start to notice the danger and the feel of tension.

Jawee and Nelo try to calm the Robinson family. They are terrified and Clifford has carefully installed a seatbelt on everyone. He puts the lap belt low across the hips below the stomach and the shoulder belt nicely tight, over the collar bone, away from the neck like he's learnt from a rescue training course he took in college.

CRAAR

The ship continues to wobble violently from side to side. Nelo watches for everyone's safety while Jawee decides to go take a look outside and find out how severe the storm is. The winds are so powerful he struggles to walk around. The door slams behind him due to pressure from the wind's thrust.

Mama Esmelda is under water looking at the ship. Although the water is very agitated, it doesn't seem to affect her. Impressively, she can swim and move around it very easily. Jawee on the other hand goes through great lengths and nearly dies trying to get back on his floor. Mama Esmelda raises her arms towards the ship. Suddenly a water sprout starts a spiral pattern on the water surface. It spins as it moves up the surface, then more than one occurs in the same vicinity. The boat staggers and bubbles of air come out of the water. With one loud sound the waves in the water stop abruptly and the ship stands still. Thanks to Mama Esmelda, the crew and everyone on board are safe. The storm clears miraculously.

Alas no one knows the reason why the sea has calmed down, but they are thankful and their fears are over. Mama Esmelda finally feels ready to reveal herself to her grandsons. The tension in the room quiets down and Rose has respiratory problems from the shock. Kia hugs her and keeps her company. It seems order is restored and the ship should make it to its destination.

To everyone's surprise they spot water leaking under the door. It gradually creates a puddle of water inside the room. A small pool of water vibrates and trembles while everyone watches. The water transforms into Mama Esmelda in front of everyone's eyes. They all look at her in astonishment. She appears in the center of the room with a greeting smile aimed at Jawee and Nelo. They recognize her familiar face and jump up and rise suddenly with excitement. That's when it becomes clear to everyone that she is responsible for the dangerous crushing waves ceasing.

"I must warn you my children," says Mama Esmelda. "The future of earth and the secret world of Tikki is in danger. I've been tormented for nights with visions of you boys. You hold the faith of our worlds in your hands, my dreams have showed me. You must train rigorously and prepare yourself for a great battle. Death will visit every city, every town and every village. Our ancestors have long warned us about these days. The scribes have written about the legends of the five creatures and left it on the walls of their shrines. If humans traverse the land of Laska, they will trespass and release this apocalyptic event on both our worlds."

"We accept the challenge!" says Jawee with firm affirmation.

These courageous boys are willing to risk their lives for their friends and the world. They have grown accustomed to the world of Kia and are now fond of its people. The allure of the music and many games they've discovered has changed their lives. They now consider this world their second home. The love they share with the Robinson family is apparent to Mama Esmelda.

With a commanding presence she reveals to Clifford and Rose that they are under surveillance by a spy. He's been following them with close observation for days. She lost sight of him but kept pursuing, close watch on the group. Frantic stares are the reaction she gets from Clifford and Rose, creating a chaotic atmosphere in the room.

"Mr. Pho!" shouts Clifford in dismay for lack of discernment. His words echo from all directions of the chamber, then the sound gradually makes it into the ears of Axo which work like a recording device. He is far from everyone, located in a storage room well-hidden on board the ship.

"You've done well Cliff; I thank you for protecting my grandsons," says Mama Esmelda in hopes to encourage him.

"You're welcome," says Lexton with sarcasm because that comment was clearly not addressed to him. No one finds his joke funny and continue on to ignore him.

Lexton cracks a bottle of rum open, unbothered and with a shrug says, "Forget y'all".

Time elapses and hours go by with Mama Esmelda in a meeting with the group. They take their time to consult with her about the future of mankind in hopes to find a solution. Cliff is merely a human being with no superpowers but wishes to fight alongside his friends Jawee and Nelo. He wants his wife Rose and his daughter Kia to remain somewhere safe once the ship gets to shore. He believes he and his brother Lexton will be able to help guide them discreetly back home to their world.

Meanwhile his brother has already finished drinking the entire bottle of rum to himself and is now passed out with drool flowing out of his mouth. Kia is ashamed of her uncle and desperately tries to wake him up all while murmuring so as to not alert Mama Esmelda. Upon sunrise when the blue sea is calm and the smog has disappeared the clear skies reveal some land a few hundred miles away. The captain enthusiastically observes the horizon with a telescope. One of his crew members on board the ship reports to him that they have a few members missing.

A horrifying scene shows Axo the robot murdering previously a few men inside the storage room. Axo is detached of all feelings and completely ruthless; he has a mission and has been programmed to follow every order precisely until the objective is completed. He's done it to avoid any unwanted attention. An eerie squeaking noise is coming from a sector of the storage room. It's Axo covering up all traces of himself before he fades away in the shadows.

"May I have your attention please? Ladies and gentlemen, I'd like to direct your attention to the television monitors. We will be showing our safety demonstration and would like the next few minutes of your complete attention says the captain of the ship on the microphone. Attention please! This is your captain with an important announcement. I repeat this is your captain with an important announcement. There is no immediate danger to our passengers or the ship and there is no reason to be alarmed but for safety reasons we request all passengers to go to their assembly stations on deck and wait there for further instructions."

A group of heroes hear the message from marine speakers. Mama Esmelda nods at everyone with a smile and then metamorphoses into a pool of water. She flows her way by the window and vanishes. A string of bizarre things have happened on the ship, but the captain has no idea there is something far more sinister than he thought possible. Many more of his men come up missing while passengers are traveling to the assembly deck.

"Oh Lord"! Oh Lord!" The crowd screams in large numbers overflowing the assembly stations. The captain starts a countdown, placing a few men on the task of re-registering every passenger on board. A sudden blaring sound is heard from everyone. Axo is seen crashing into barrels powerfully. Mama Esmelda emerges in the crowd disguised as a regular old woman. The crowd stares in amazement at the broken robot, watching sparks ignite from his convulsing body.

Jawee and Nelo witness the whole thing accompanied by Clifford and his family. The captain and security team rush to the scene. They do not know the perpetrator, but it was Mama Esmelda who destroyed the robot. She stood with a glare, locking eyes with Jawee and Nelo then slowly disappeared in the crowd. It was clear now that they were being followed by the Doorcom Corporation and this robot bears the logo.

CHAPTER 6

The captain's crew investigates the surroundings and snoops around Axo the robot before they salvage most of his parts. Something strange is going on but nobody knows its roots. People eventually re attend their rooms and everything gets back to normal. In solitude Jawee is recharging his power sitting and meditating. Nelo and Lexton are playing catch with Loco and Simka, throwing a rubber ball back and forth. They seem to have fun. Clifford on the other hand is browsing a map planning the route they should take once they exit the ship.

Now Rose is doing Kia's hair in the bedroom while they watch TV. Everything seems to be fine and the night is falling. On the lower deck there is a site for the disposal of waste materials. Some pieces of Axo's body have been dumped there. His broken breastplate mysteriously starts to wobble all alone by itself among the rubbish. A miniscule Axo the robot rises from out the rubble.

"Master, mission failed, moving forward with mission number two", says Axo to Mr. Pho, listening from his laboratory.

Mr. Pho ponders stressfully as he observes and keeps watch. Will his master plan work or did he underestimate Clifford and the two boys? Only time will tell but so far our heroes have been lucky.

The ship held its course and now it's finally prepared to dock. Once the ship arrives at the destination the passengers are discharged from their vessels. Departures and arrivals meet at this border here in West Africa. Our friends follow the exit and begin a new part of their journey. A very long road is ahead of them before they get close to the area known to lead to Laska. Of course not only will they have to rent a jeep but a long way down the road they will need to get horses due to the harsh terrain.

They find a small hostel nearby and decide to camp there for the night. It's a small rural area on the banks of a river populated by villagers selling merchandise of all sorts. Some people sell exotic spices, others fish of different shapes and sizes. Many walk around begging in the market next to booths that sell fabric. Cliff books two rooms at the entrance for his friends and family. Unfortunately for him, he gets harassed by the villagers on his way to carry his luggage. A crippled man in a wheelchair with a young boy follows him, imploring him earnestly to help. He falls short of disregarding them and has pity. They offer some help with his luggage in return for a little bit of change. Clifford accepts and they carry his belongings to his room. With a lot of struggle they succeed in dropping it off. Our friends sojourn for a day and rest here for a night.

The next morning Clifford awakens to his alarm clock a bit worn out. Everyone seems to be sleeping so Clifford quietly gets up out his bed while Rose snores a few times. He slips in new clothes and walks out to go venture in the village. The long trip has made him hungry so he goes searching for some food. Roaming around he finds a small market that has sweet smells. When he reaches for his wallet his mouth drops. The wallet is no longer in his pocket. Clifford panics and runs back to his room hoping he must have misplaced it somewhere.

When he eventually arrives in the room, he advises everyone to search for their belongings. That's when they find out they all have been robbed. The money is all gone and it dawns on Clifford that it was the crippled man in the wheelchair and the young boy with him that stole everything. A very clever scheme these thieves have put together. Perhaps the villagers' usually target tourists and were able to recognize our friends' unfamiliar faces. Feeling like a fool, Clifford is furious but he refuses to relinquish. He storms out the room and goes searching for the thieves.

It's a small town and people may know the pickpockets. Perhaps they shouldn't be far.

Few hours go by as Cliff undertakes an investigation but ends with no avail. Passing by the markets he notices a few flyers all around town. The flyers are showcasing an ultimate fighting tournament, offering a big cash prize to whoever is able to win the challenge. The tournament is held today and it invites people of all fighting styles. You can spar with a wide variety of opponents that are all fearless and strong. Combining elements of boxing, kickboxing, Muay Thai, wrestling, and Jiu Jitsu with many more fighting skills.

"Twenty five thousand for the winner!" says Clifford inquisitively.

He is well aware that he and his family are in for trouble and are stuck in a deep hole. They lost all their money and have no means to continue traveling. This tournament may be the only answer to everyone's problems. Cliff thinks about it then continues to read the flyer. All fighters are expected to display skill and control. This is a martial art tournament and all fighters are expected to conduct themselves with respect for the weapon, their opponents and the tournament staff. Any fighter that is deemed to pose danger to themselves or others, excessive force/illegal targeting, etc. will be addressed at the discretion of the tournament director.

The tournament director will serve as the ultimate authority within the ring. The disciplinary procedure will generally constitute first warning, then a penalty. Then an expulsion from the match or tournament, however, this procedure shall remain at the discretion of the director. Fighters who have been banned from attendance at other tournaments are not permitted to attend the combat.

As in previous years the most prestigious price for all participants is the sportsmanship prize for twenty five thousand dollars. All rounds will be ninety seconds. The clock will not stop unless there is an equipment timeout or an injury time out. While Cliff is holding the flyer a very odd coincidence happens right before his eyes. He spots the crippled old man walking. No longer crippled but instead is agile and strong. This old thief is spotted by Clifford from far away. Nonchalantly he is seen strolling past and entering the entrance of the tournament.

"Got ya!" screams Clifford.

Instead of rushing on the opportunity, Cliff makes a smart move.

He goes to gather the crew for help and comes up with a plan. If he joins the tournament he can serve as a decoy while everyone else looks for the old thief in the crowd of spectators and besides, who knows if he might be able to win the cash prize. The search begins and everyone is onboard except Rose who disagrees and is not sure if Cliff should go to combat, she finds it risky. He is prepared mentally and physically already, Cliff watches everyone with a calm look void of anxiety. Jawee and Nelo are inspired by it and their skin illuminates faintly. You can hear the noise of the footsteps of a crowd gathering and loud punching and kicking exchanges coming from the tournament. A loud "Hurray" from people shouting in excitement the gates open and our group of friends enter the tournament.

"Welcome to The Akan Battle of the South" says the gatekeeper, giving blessings and wishing luck to all of the challengers who dare to enter the ring.

Many challengers are injured and can no longer fight because they couldn't succumb to the blows from the one fighter they call the Slasher. Many are fearful and quit the competition because of him. Cliff jumps above the ropes and enters the ring when his name is called. Standing on a wood plank he starts shadow boxing before the match for practice.

CHAPTER 7

They carry out the plan as promised and put it into action. Our friends separate to start searching for the crippled old thief and his young partner in the crowd. Cliff launches an onslaught of attacks, disabling his first opponent. He surprises everyone, not only the large crowd but his friends as well. They cheer his name and the judges pronounce him winner of the match. The crippled old man is nowhere to be found until the gatekeeper calls out to battle a man well known for his battling skills and agility.

"And on stage now to battle Mr. Lemba! " says the gatekeeper with a loud voice.

The fighter who stands in the ring bears a resemblance to the crippled old man but instead of being crippled he is very agile. He devastates each challenger they send to him, making the one they call the Slasher anxious to fight him. The crew realizes it is indeed the crippled old thief. Although he is a thief, his greed brought him to the tournament in hopes of getting some extra cash. After a few fights the judges place Mr. Lemba and Clifford neck and neck. They will have to fight to move on to the next level and challenge the champion.

"You thief I found you!" exclaims Clifford.

The old man shies away and puts his head down. Now furious, Clifford hops into the ring which he has gladly anticipated. The looks on Jawee and Nelo's faces are astonished and they signal all the others to watch what is about to transpire. From a far way above the stadium is a tiny little robot that is hovering above the scene. Indeed Axo the robot is watching and transmitting the whole entire match to Mr. Pho. Mr. Pho doesn't know what to make of this and prefers not to inform Mr. Ford of anything.

Cliff launches an attack, he swings at his opponent but the old man avoids each one easily. This dance goes on for three rounds and Cliff is unable to touch Mr. Lemba. The old man finally speaks and tells Cliff "I'm sorry for what I did to you guys. You would not understand."

In one motion he dashes towards Cliff and strikes him in his rib with a roundhouse kick. Then proceed to give him a reverse neck choke, making him go to sleep. The old man cannot be underestimated and the judges stop the fight. The plan has failed, not only will Cliff not have a chance to win the cash prize but now the old man has humiliated him and stands a chance to get away.

Rose escorts Clifford off the ring with the help of Lexton. Seems like all is lost for the group and their spirit is broken. On the contrary for Nelo, he is unmoved. He convinces Jawee to join the tournament with him.

"You must not give away your identities", says Kia to the boys.

"She is right because the future of our worlds is in jeopardy", responds Cliff.

There is no other option, the boys concluded. So they take action and register their names in the Akan tournament. The judges and a few men in the crowd laugh at Jawee and Nelo when they see them enter the competition. They are clearly no match to the big and skillful combatants, especially the one they call the Slasher. The judges call to fight Nelo first and he winks at Jawee then enters the ring. The swiftness and agility Nelo demonstrates baffles everyone. The crowd goes silent. He completely dominates his opponent then pretends to sleep on stage, mocking his challenger who lays unconscious from Nelo's last assault. The matches go on and Jawee likewise shows a superb performance. This causes the crowd to cheer in multitudes making a noise so loud that it vibrates the stadium.

Mr. Lemba the pronounce thief is called to challenge Jawee.

This is the moment Cliff and his family have been waiting for.

"Prepare to meet your match," says Jawee authoritatively.

The old man doesn't answer but instead takes a fighting stance. A series of acrobatic kicks and punches are exchanged. First a butterfly kick from Jawee that gets blocked by Mr. Lemba. Then a cross hook and a jab from the old man gets dodged by Jawee. The flexibility and speed demonstrated by Jawee is a sight to behold. The old thief cannot keep pace with the boy but somehow is able to duck and avert all attacks. The battle continues as spectators chant and watch. They can't seem to hit each other, but unfortunately for the old man eventually his endurance is depleted. Mr. Lemba is brave and withstands the onslaught, but he is now weak and full of sweat. A young boy in the midst of the crowd screams "Stop the fight!" Then he goes on to throw a white towel in the ring. The young boy takes a hold of the old weak man and carries him offstage.

"Uncle, why did you join?" says the boy.

"I had to for Sarah," answers the old man with a faint voice.

This was the young boy that was pushing the wheelchair for the old crippled thief. He recognizes Clifford and Lexton. Together they approach and confront the thieves.

"We are sorry for our actions," says the young boy. "You do not understand, this old man here is my uncle and he's done nothing but help me and my mother. She is very ill and overwhelmed with affliction. Because she isn't able to work and is confined to her bed, we can't afford her medicine and proper treatment from a doctor. That's the reason why my uncle and I went out to steal. Please forgive us," pleads the young boy to Clifford and Lexton.

The ashamed old man also submits himself and pleads for forgiveness. Clifford and Lexton are moved by their actions and reconcile.

"We understand and appreciate your honesty. Although it's wrong what you did, we would do anything to help a loved one as well," says Clifford.

They gather together with the group and there they make peace with each other. The competition must go on because regrettably for our crew, their only hope is in this tournament.

"I promise I will win and share the prize to help your mother" says Nelo with confidence.

Nelo captures the crowd and wins the heart of everyone. He creates tension amongst the fighters, making the Slasher furious and ready to fight with him. Jawee and Nelo defeat all challengers, leaving them with only the Slasher left. The judge's decree for Nelo to fight next. He waves at the crowd and does acrobatic dances to entertain them. The Slasher responds by banging his chest twice to scare him and win the crowd back. He's angry and has a ferocious way of fighting his opponents. The Slasher wants all the attention and will stop at nothing to win. Nelo on the other hand smirks and laughs at the Slasher and is not scared at all.

"I'm going to make you prostrate yourself and honor me, you little weakling" says the Slasher.

"1, 2, 3, FIGHT!" Shouts, the referee and the match begins.

The Slasher storms towards Nelo violently. The impact makes him almost fly out of the ring. Nelo gets up painfully then takes a fighting stance. His body illuminates a little. Jawee signals him not to use his super powers. He ceases immediately and instead launches a spectacular attack.

The Slasher is robust and has a long range, but even his advantage could not protect him from the speed and aggressiveness of Nelo.

By the third round his face is no longer recognizable and he is blind in one eye. The judges call to stop the match and declare Nelo the winner. The Slasher strongly disapproves of this and argues with them. He breaks a few chains and tables forcing the judges to have him escorted out of the stadium.

With no more challengers left, the judges call Jawee and Nelo to fight for the championship. Jawee in return steps down and quits, leaving Nelo as the champion. Glamour and cheers commence and the crowd celebrates. The boys are viewed as champions in the eyes of the people. Nelo receives the cash prize of the Akan battle of the South from the judges, and then regroups with his friends. Nelo flaunts his trophy to Jawee as if to taunt him but Jawee gives him a grimace.

CHAPTER 8

All is won, fortunately and for everyone there is hope. Peace is restored and they have more than enough money now. The two boys adhere to generosity and gladly approach the old man with his nephew. Nelo offers a part of the cash prize to Mr. Lemba to make sure Sarah; his ill mother, gets the proper treatment and medical care. In return Mr. Lemba almost breaks out in tears and is very pleased. He blesses our group of friends and so does the little boy with him. His mother is very ill and he feared the worst for her. Mr. Lemba refuses to leave everyone without offering his help in return for the gift.

"I can help you travel wherever you want to go", says the old man. "I know every inch and crevice of this land and I've traveled throughout the whole continent".

Delighted, Cliff has an agreeable reaction to his words. The old man can be trusted and certainly can be a help to everyone. He knows the wildlife and the landscape and the dangers that lie ahead. He bids his nephew farewell and insists that he takes care of all that his ill mother requires. The quest to get the boys to Laska continues but this time this is where the trip ends for the Robinson family. Only Clifford will be taking the mysterious children back to their homeland. No one must know the whereabouts of Laska, not even Clifford. But he will be allowed to take them to the same, initial place where they first met. Cliff has kept the memoirs of its location but without a crew and the proper equipment, it's a dangerous journey.

Kia offers her help by opening the bird cage and handing Loco and Simka to Jawee. It's going to be a perilous safari. Perhaps they can be helpful. Before the voyage Jawee and Nelo depart and separate from the group to go meditate and recharge. They climb up a giant tree and sit motionless with their eyes closed. A faint luminous green light radiates from their skin. They stay suspended on the tree and remain in that manner for one hour to completely regenerate. Shrouded in mystery, no one knows the secrets that the inhabitants of Tikki are hiding. That strange place full of valleys and rivers with mountains unseen by mankind, ancient ruins show mythical tales of a bridge between our world and Tikki.

Some villagers claim there are portals in different parts of the world leading to these unknown places. Some in Asia, some in India and some you can find here in Africa. Many have tried finding its whereabouts but no one has ever succeeded. Throughout the ages people have searched for it but eventually its stories and its fame faded away. People stopped believing in fairy tales and ancient folklore stories. Life ran its course and history took away the knowledge.

   A camera lens zooms in on Jawee and Nelo before the camera flashes a few times. Kia tries to capture the moment and save a souvenir of her new friends. They wish each other a cheerful farewell before departure. Now that the Robinson family has had enough provision, they are safe to temporarily reside here in the continent of Africa, away from the agents of Doorcom. They wish to further go south towards Tanzania and settle near the border to wait for Clifford there.

Lexton, on the contrary, has become accustomed to the Akan village and he's cleverly bamboozled everyone there into believing that he has trained Jawee and Nelo with their fighting skills. He somehow has convinced everyone he is a coach and now they revere him. People support him and willingly become his student. Even the judges of the Akan tournament provide him with a class and a hall to teach. Everybody has seen what Jawee and Nelo can do and they all wish to fight like that one day.

Lexton is always up to something and he is living the ride. He says to everyone with a smile that he will be staying in the village. Mr. Lemba escorts Clifford and the strange boys with a busted old jeep wrangler. It's an old car that he loves and is attached to, although it doesn't perform well. It's very rusty and emits a cringey sound when he turns on the ignition. Something Mr. Lemba does before he invites the crew to hop in. They drive across a long desert and lots of rocky terrain before reaching a pit stop. The place is actually a cul de sac and there is no more road or possibility for a car to venture. Mr. Lemba steps out of the car to seemingly go examine the dead end, but instead he reaches into the woods and steps back out with three horses.

"They will help us from here," says Mr. Lemba to Cliff.

Cliff has no experience and doesn't know how to ride horses but grabs his saddle instinctively. He hands a horse to Jawee and offers the second to Nelo. The answer surprises everyone because they refuse and prefer to travel by foot. Cliff clutches onto a picture of him and Rose and kisses it. It's a picture he usually carries with him everywhere he goes. His wife Rose is a very beautiful woman. She has a bright smile and very pretty eyes. She's elegant and graceful which is why Kia tries to dress like her sometimes.

Cliff struggles to mount the horse although it's a trained one. Jawee and Nelo laugh at him as they stand there and watch the funny spectacle. Mr. Lemba decides to help him up before he gets discouraged. The sun sets on our crew as they travel through a valley full of vegetation and great lakes. Loco and Simka disappear in the forest in the midst of all this beauty. Wild animals of all sorts continue their day to day activities in their habitat undisturbed by human influence.

Soon, Cliff realizes that he isn't so safe in this ecosystem when he gets near the lake to fetch for some water in order to cool off. A crocodile rises from the water to gobble up Cliff, the visitor. He was quietly watching underwater, ready to hunt him down. Luckily for Cliff, Jawee wasn't too far and spotted the predator. When the crocodile jumps to launch his fatal attack he gets bombarded with plants in the shape of arrows, piercing his eyes and inside his mouth in a very gruesome manner.

Jawee can survive easily in this landscape; he fits right in this habitat.

Laska has its share of ferocious beasts much more dangerous than our normal world. Cliff almost catches a heart attack and trembles for a few minutes after the event still in shock. Nelo finds it amusing and this gets him excited. He vanishes in the forest and goes hunting. A little bit of food for the trip wouldn't hurt. Still observing from a safe distance lies Axo the robot. He does manage to follow them unnoticeably in the valley.

As they draw near their destination and reach the point where Clifford found the boys initially, Axo sends signals to alarm Mr. Pho, his master. Yes, indeed, Mr. Lemba will have to part ways. He has successfully helped the group get to where they had to go. He will have to cross the valley and back track in his steps to his jeep wrangler. It's time to offer his farewell. He salutes everyone with kind wishes before mounting his horse. The journey is long and bumpy as our heroes continue closer and closer to reach their destination. Loco appears from a tree-top flying towards Jawee. He lands on his shoulder.

"I found Laska!" he says.

A Christ like feeling of comfort comes into Jawee when he hears this. Alas, good news has come and they have successfully made it back safely. Well at least so they think but unfortunately not so far away, Axo has kept on their trail. He activates a program that scans the landscape. Trouble awaits for our heroes; they underestimated Mr. Ford's and Doorcom. Mr. Ford trustee apprentice Mr. Pho is a clever one and never fails an assignment.

Cliff is unaware and is getting ready to finally say his goodbyes to the boys. They have appointed Simka to lead their way back to civilization. Jawee and Nelo thank him with their utmost respect. They will miss him and miss this world but it's time to get back home. There are faint noises of wildlife and the sound of wind blowing on the trees while Jawee and Nelo disappear into bushes.

A few days pass and Cliff is reunited with his family. All is well and the weather is quite nice. Everything is back to normal in the world of the Robinsons.

In another location away from the busy cities. You can find Axo in full grown size accompanied by men wearing Doorcom uniforms. They are treading along the site that borders our world and Laska. Yes indeed to our horror they have found the mythical land of Laska. Mr. Pho is on-scene also sharing this discovery. Before Doorcom can celebrate, a powerful shock wave hits the terrain. The vibration shatters a few trees and mountains nearby. Some sort of electrical current traverses through the ground heading through a portal. The sparks found their way to the waters where lies, the legendary sleeping creatures.

A small hand movement is made by one creature. A sound of cataclysmic proportion is heard in both worlds. The waters start to recede and drain the region. Soon the world will have to face these creatures. The waters slowly go down, revealing a portion of the heads of those enigmatic creatures. Psychics from all over the world are weakened by the event. Axo the robot, Mr. Pho and the few men from Doorcom are transmuted by the current of energy. They gradually start to change form.

Moist air rises and a cloud forms, building a thunder storm of massive size. The catacombs of the legendary creatures now are covered with debris. Scattered pieces of waste remains now surround the site.

Four warriors from Mulon wearing gold plates are summoned by the scribes to prepare for battle. Mama Esmelda is amongst them as chief advisor leading an army. Jawee and Nelo awaken from meditation with rays of light inside a crystal palace.

In the meantime the Robinsons are having a lovely day. Rose is cleaning up the bird cage and feeding treats to Loco and Simka. Clifford is helping Kia build a Go kart powered by a two-stroke engine.

"Sir the crew is not responsive!" Mr. Ford looks at his personnel and draws a blank stare.

All systems are shut down and there is no sign of Mr. Pho and his crew. What will happen to the future of mankind? Are Jawee and Nelo prepared to face the five creatures of the world? Will the creatures be merciful or will they wreak havoc?

Jawee and Nelo arrive before the army. They witness the thunderstorms and the clouds covering the sky. The river is now empty and completely drained. The two boys find no sign of movement under the debris. The colossal creatures are motionless, perhaps trapped beneath the rocks as a suspenseful silence envelopes the site.

At a short distance not so far away, Mama Esmelda is seen accompanied by a great army from Mulon. Generals from different parts of Tikki have joined to be allies against the creatures. The golden kingdom in Mulon hides weapons unimaginable to the common man. This army is well equipped for the gathering with golden shields and golden swords. The storm calms down and the lightning stops roaring. Jawee and Nelo approach the site and begin to dig. They amass huge rubble and try to clear the area.

While in action, they look at each other and encourage themselves to have no fear and continue on. Mama Esmelda is impressed by their bravery and is proud of her grandsons. Standing twenty feet tall overlooks the creatures inert. They look lifeless without any threat. Nelo decides to hit one to get a reaction. These mechanical creatures seem to not be functional. A large crowd of soldiers from Mulon grab hold of shackles and begin to tie up the creatures and hold them down. They restrain them safely with no trouble. This was a false alarm according to the elders. Mama Esmelda advises the assembly to secure the area before she raises her hands to use her powers. Water starts to gush forth from the rocks in the mountains, slowly recreating the river.

"No one from mankind has entered the portal", states an official.

"Let's guard the gates and release magic on the other side to make mankind unable to see this location", says the elders.

Jawee and Nelo's stories are heard in all of the kingdoms and they become famous.

Meanwhile in the forest not so far away, one man from Doorcom rises and wakes up, immediately after Mr. Pho awakens with a huge headache. Everyone's memory seems to be unclear as if the storm was just a dream. Axo's built-in camera has lost all the data that identifies Mr. Pho when he activates him. This is terrible news for everyone because the mission failed. Mr. Pho will have to pay for all the expenses and damages done. He will also have to deal with the judgment of Mr. Ford. The Staff of Doorcom pack up and leave to return home. They return to society and get back to their families and friends.

Back in Canada in a small town, the city is buzzing with traffic lights and cars drifting. Mr. Pho is seated right next to a bartender asking for a second round of shot glasses. He looks depressed and beat up because of his failure to find Laska. He drowns himself with alcohol in hopes to cover his shame. With a deranged look he keeps asking himself where he has gone wrong. Once he gobbles one more shot, he gags and becomes nauseous.

"Hey buddy! The bathroom is over there!" says the bartender who tries to avoid a mess.

Mr. Pho almost throws up on his way to the bathroom. The aftermath is not a pretty sight but he later on feels better. In the bathroom Mr. Pho eventually goes to clean up and approaches the sink. He wipes his face with a napkin and stares at himself in the mirror. Suddenly he hears a voice calling him. When he turns around he finds nobody there. The voice calls him one more time and again the same results. No one is in the bathroom with him but yet he hears a voice.

"I am Barak, one of the legendary creatures of Laska," the voice said.

Mr. Pho is stunned and falls to his feet.

THE END